The Bandaged

The Empyrean Saga Book Two

Steve Stred

Black Void Publishing

Cover by Ross Jeffery

Contents

1. The Empyrean Saga Series — 1

2. Advance Praise — 3

3. ABOVE — 5

4. 0. Class — 7

5. 1. Before — 11

6. 2. — 13

7. 3. — 15

8. 4. — 17

9. 5. — 23

10. 6. — 27

11. 7. — 29

12. 8. — 31

13. 9. — 33

14. 10. GREY — 35

15. 11. — 41

16.	12.	43
17.	13.	47
18.	14.	49
19.	15.	51
20.	16.	53
21.	17. Thompson	55
22.	18.	59
23.	19.	63
24.	20.	65
25.	21.	69
26.	22.	71
27.	23. Jettisoned	73
28.	24.	77
29.	25.	79
30.	26.	83
31.	27. Progress	85
32.	28.	87
33.	29.	91
34.	30.	93
35.	31.	95
36.	32.	99
37.	33. Silo	101

38. 34.	103
39. 35.	105
40. 36. Solution	109
41. 37. The Visit	113
42. 38.	117
43. 39. Arrival	121
44. About the Author	129

The Empyrean Saga Series

Book 1: The Future In the Sky
Book 2: The Bandaged
Book 3: The Devourers
Book 4: The Returned
Book 5: Where All Light Ends
Book 6: An Orange Sky Shines Down (The Empyrean Saga Poetry Companion)

<h1>Advance Praise</h1>

"'The Future In the Sky' is a compelling literary treat – wholly original, surprising and ultimately moving. I'd recommend it to anyone."

-Tim Lebbon, HWA Bram Stoker Award winning author, author of 'The Silence,' 'Eden' and 'Relics.'

"Reminiscent of Bradbury, The Future in the Skies is an intimate, character-driven exploration of coming of age in a grim future. Dread builds from the first chapter and doesn't let up."

- Laurel Hightower, author of Crossroads

"I was only three pages in when I knew this story would be one I read in a single sitting. A sci-fi work of dystopian existence driven by Lizzie's gut-wrenching fear and a need for the truth. Steve Stred's characters jump from the pages, becoming part of your world, causing you to care what happens. Stred doesn't waste a single sentence in this must-read novella."

- Cindy O'Quinn, HWA Bram Stoker Award nominated author of Lydia

"Steve Stred has presented a tale of surreal, dark science-fiction here that asks questions of place and

belonging, of duty and desire, and might leave you questioning your own choices... or lack of them."
   - Alan Baxter, award-winning author of Devouring Dark and Served Cold
   "The Future In the Sky' proves Stred can't be restrained by genre"
   - Gavin Kendall, Kendall Reviews

ABOVE

"T-Minus ten seconds..."

The family gathered around the television, watching excitedly as the countdown reached zero and the Empyrean ship launched from Earth.

'Mr. Eldridge is a true hero,' the dad said, clapping his son on the back.

They all remained fixated on the screen as the ship travelled further and further away from the surface, growing closer to its destination above the planet.

'Dad, will we get to live up there?' the daughter asked.

'Afraid not,' he replied. 'We've been chosen as Inhabitors. We were selected to remain behind and if we survive the event, we'll work to make the planet liveable for humans once again. Some have called us the true heroes."

His son rolled his eyes. They weren't heroes, they were sacrifices.

Above the planet, the ship slowed before arriving at the coordinates that would allow it to orbit the Earth for the rest of its existence.

0. Class

He greeted the morning like every other one living on this godforsaken place.

With anger, rage and bitterness.

The older he got the longer it took to wake. Sitting on the edge of the bed was a chore. Standing more so. If he had the ability to operate a motorized chair he'd do it in a heartbeat, but that simply wasn't possible here.

Shuffling into the kitchen of the rundown house, he examined the level of fuel that remained in the small generator. Tapped the gauge once, twice, hoping to expel an air bubble or find it had magically increased over night. The reading showed that he'd be able to power his coffee maker long enough to make a cup, so he flipped the switch and sat down as the generator rumbled to life. He'd need to talk to Thompson about sourcing some more fuel. And coffee. He knew that the scavenger trips were taking longer and longer the more things were picked over. Soon, a day would come when the scavengers would return empty handed, or worse, not at all.

Once the machine had done its job and filled his chipped cup with dark goodness, he took a drink, savoring the flavor, even if it wasn't good. How he wished for the old days, where he'd walk to the cafeteria or café near the Research Lab and get a coffee from there. Now, he was lucky if he had coffee once a month.

Just another thing that cocksucker Eldridge took from me, he thought, finishing the cup off with a long drink. He set it down near the sink of dirty dishes. Catching his distorted reflection off one of the plates, he cringed, bringing a hand to his face. He dabbed where some of the blood had soaked through the wrappings. Making his way to the bathroom, he didn't like what he found. The bandages had unravelled during the night, a result most likely from another restless sleep where he tossed and turned. He did something he very rarely did – he completely unravelled the bandages and threw them in the bin by the unused shower. Rewrapping his head and face with new, clean bandages, he wondered just how long they'd stay pristine. *Ten minutes?* At most if he was lucky.

He glanced towards the bedroom window, finding the outside growing brighter. The sun was beginning to start its climb into the sky, which meant he needed to step it up a notch and make his way to the school.

*

The door squealed as he pushed it open and made his way into the darkened hall, the door clanging shut behind him.

The hallway was in a state of disrepair; litter and debris scattered throughout. The lockers similar. Some closed. Some open. A few still had locks on them, as though waiting for the student to return and open it.

The sound of the man walking was the only noise; the click-click of heel strikes followed by the clack of the cane hitting the floor.

He shuffled along until he arrived at his classroom. Pushing the door open with a groan, the man went to the desk at the front of the room. He tapped his cane against the top of the desk three times before speaking.

"Students, students, quiet please. Sorry for my tardiness this morning. Picking up from yesterday, let's continue. Today we'll cover chapters three to five in your text book."

Hearing something, he looked up at the empty desks. Letting out a long sigh, he sat on the dust covered chair that took up space between the chalkboard and desk.

"Please, just for once, can I get some GODDAMNED RESPECT?"

His hands found his head, tentatively cupping it with outstretched fingers. The material of the stained bandages aggravated him, but he pushed the irritation aside to rest his face in his palms.

"Is that just too much to ask?"

A rattling sound from above began, growing in intensity.

Great, acid rain. Those Empyrean scum dumping their waste water again, he thought, rage bubbling more.

Sitting silently, he looked at his imagined students, waiting for the thunderous deluge to pass. He smiled at the twins; Donny and Danny. Gave a nod to Elizabeth who sat in the back but always handed in her work on time. *If only these were real students and not fake characters I've created to try and keep me sane?*

As the rain subsided and the clouds faded, sunshine returned outside the decrepit school. The man stood, only to reposition and sit on the corner of desk.

"How about I tell you a story, yeah? Instead of going further into our studies, how about I share how the brilliant mind you see before you was exiled from *up there* and lives his life on this wretched planet, wishing for death's sweet embrace to arrive. How about that?"

More silence greeted him, which he took as an invitation to continue.

"My name is Dr. Harkins, Edward Harkins to my mother, and I used to be Albert Eldridge's right hand man."

1. Before

Walking into the Laboratory Level on the revolving ship never grew old for Dr. Edward Harkins. Eldridge had designed the perfect place for the residents to live, knowing the carnage and chaos that had ensued on earth.

He scanned in, said good morning to Emily, the medical administrator and went to the board room at the far end of the Level. He had an idea of what the day's meeting was going to cover, but his mind lingered on his experiments. Harkins lived and breathed science and adored how just one cellular shift could fundamentally change the biology of what he was working on.

"Harkins, morning," the man sitting behind the long table in the board room called out as Harkins entered.

"Morning, Albert. How are things?"

"Excellent my old friend. Most excellent. Our guest will arrive shortly. Until then, have a seat. I've already loaded some information on the retinal screens."

Harkins sat, placing the device over his head and pushed the view button. As a woman appeared on screen, he struggled to place her. He'd seen her somewhere before, but where?

Harkins focused on the images before him, watching as she discussed her research on something she referred to as 'the lightbulb.' She knew if they just found the switch and managed to turn it on, it would be a game changer for the residents who resided above the earth.

As the images ended, the boardroom door opened and the woman whom he'd just watched walked in, carrying a digital screen with her.

"Ah, Ms. Morton, please do have a seat," Eldridge said, gesturing to an empty chair.

"It's Dr. Rachel Morton, if you will."

"My apologies," Eldridge said.

Harkins saw from the look on his face that he enjoyed that she wasn't intimidated by the man who'd created and funded the revolving ship.

"Shall we start?" she asked, pulling up some holographic data.

The three dove into what she was working on and as the meeting progressed Harkins knew his research would be put on the back burner.

2.

'Daddy won't wake up.'
  'He doesn't need too.'
  'What about mommy?'
  'Look outside. None of us need to wake up. The bombs have been launched.'

3.

"It simply isn't possible," Harkins bellowed, slamming his fist onto the top of the bench where he was working. The microscope he'd been using clattered and tipped over, the sample on the slide skidding off the surface and smashing on the floor.

"Harkins, whoa, whoa," Morton called out, coming over from her own work station. "Easy there. What's going on?"

"Don't *easy there*, me," he said, standing in rage. Ever since she'd wormed into Eldridge's good graces he'd been pushed further and further away from his research.

"Hey now. I just want to help. You've seen the data. You know what I've proposed is possible."

"I did and I do. But the equipment currently I'm trying to use just can't handle the details. I need to zoom in even more on the microscopic level. We've been working on this for close to a year and we've made absolutely no progress."

"Let's discuss this with Albert? I'm sure they're working on something on the Research Level that'll be able to aid us?"

He hated when she talked down to him, as though he was a child. His temper was flaring, anger rising. She sensed it.

"Harkins. You know we're a team. I can't do this without you. You're brilliant. Eldridge needs us on the same page. Ok?"

He nodded. It took everything in his power to not stab her in the neck.

4.

The Research Level was one Harkins had never had the privilege of visiting before.

This was Eldridge's prized level. When he'd fled into space on the ship, all of his earthly research had been collected and placed here.

Even though Harkins was one of the lead research scientists on board, he wasn't an engineer nor a robotics expert. Different skills on different levels was the mantra Eldridge had drilled into every single person living on the ship, no matter how much it pissed Harkins off and felt like he was being belittled.

He remained silent as they travelled up the elevator of the revolving ship. When they came to a stop on the level and the doors opened, Harkins couldn't help but gasp at what awaited them.

This was his Nirvana.

Morton walked ahead of him, scanning her ID card and motioning for him to hurry up. He closed his mouth and rushed over.

"Eldridge gave you temporary access. Not sure for how long, but scan in so that the level will allow your presence."

He placed his ID card under the scanner and watched as his data appeared on the screen and a red flashing bar indicated he was permitted.

The glass doors slid open and they walked in. Almost immediately Harkins stumbled. Looking, he saw that the walk way undulated and the metal panels shifted and reformed.

A short, muscular woman wearing all white approached and smiled.

"Welcome to the Research and Development Level. Mr. Eldridge has asked that while here, you do not touch anything unless it has to specifically do with your own necessity. As you've already discovered, the level is AI. The floors are a living entity on its own right. From what Dr. Morton has mentioned in setting this up, what you two possibly need will be right this way, if you'll follow me."

Harkins was stunned.

As they started to walk he saw things being worked on that he couldn't even fathom.

"Are we permitted to ask any questions?" he asked.

"You may, but I may or may not be permitted to answer them," the woman replied.

"Fair enough. Is this where the original orbs were produced?"

Judging by her reaction, Harkins hazarded a guess that she hadn't expected that question. She turned, smiling.

"What an excellent question and one never asked. Yes, in fact this is where Mr. Eldridge himself first developed the orbs to facilitate individual's new and improved futures."

"I'd love to see the machine that was used. He's spoken of it to me previously, but it would be an honor to actually see it."

"We do have it here. It is in special storage. While you're examining the equipment I'll contact Mr. Eldridge and see if that can be arranged."

As they continued walking, Harkins tried to make as many mental notes as he could. While he wasn't planning anything with this knowledge, he found that you never knew when a bit of information may help overcome a road block.

The space was nothing short of impressive. When they finally arrived at the area that housed microscopic research, Harkins estimated he'd seen over one hundred projects with over three hundred researchers hard at work.

The future of the ship and their progress was in great hands.

"Here we go," the woman said, stepping aside so that they could enter. "While you two meet with Dr. Williams, I'll go contact Mr. Eldridge."

Before them stood a man close to seven feet tall. He was wearing glasses and a smile on his face that made Harkins believe he must've been from European descent.

"Dr. Morton, a pleasure as always," he said, shaking her hand. He turned and smiled at Harkins. "Dr. Edward Harkins. A true pleasure. To think, the man responsible for the entire Medical Level of the Empyrean revolving ship is standing before me. You may not know this, but you saved my mother when I was very little."

They shook hands.

"I did not know this. Please, tell me more. My apologies."

Dr. Williams gave a wave that said not to worry about it.

"When I was five, my mother developed an embolism. Or at least they thought it was. She was a retired Returner. It was believed that she hadn't decompressed correctly at some point. You were the one who ultimately arrived when she went into Cardiac Arrest and determined it was a blood infection."

"That's right. I do remember that. She'd been exposed to something on the surface on her last expedition and when she came back it attacked her system."

"You got her stabilized and you created an anti-biotic in less than thirty minutes and she was good as new by that night."

"Thirty minutes?" Morton asked, in utter shock.

"Yes. I took a guess at what she'd been exposed to. Actually, it was a calculated guess. I saw on her helmet a green smudge and presumed it was one of the mutated poisonous plants that have reclaimed most of the former Mediterranean area of the surface."

"You're saving her propelled me into a life of science. Along the way I fell in love with the engineering side of things. And now, voila, head of the Research and Development Level."

"Head of the Level! Well congratulations to you, Dr. Williams. And I'm humbled to have played a small role in your journey."

"Yes, well, should we begin?" Morton cut in, annoyance evident.

The three went over to the table that took up the center of the space. Upon it was a number of contraptions. Over the next few hours, Dr. Williams went through their capabilities while quizzing the duo on what exactly they were requiring. When all was said and done, Harkins was confident that the third microscopic examiner that Dr. Williams had modified for them would work just fine.

As they were finishing up, the woman returned.

"Mr. Eldridge says that you're able to visit the machine, Dr. Harkins. He'll meet you there in less than five minutes."

That caught the three off guard.

"Mr. Eldridge is coming here? To my level?" Dr. Williams said.

"Has he never been?" Dr. Morton replied.

"No, never. I do video conferences with him and I've been to the main Board Level a few times, but this is an unexpected surprise. What a privilege. May I join?"

"At this time, I'm afraid not. Mr. Eldridge had indicated that he'll be meeting with Dr. Harkins and Dr. Harkins alone."

This also caught the three by surprise.

"I'll wait for you back at the Lab Level," Morton said, leaving. Harkins heard her tone and saw how she walked away. She was not happy.

Dr. Williams meanwhile looked as though he was a kicked puppy.

"Hey, Dr. Williams. Don't take it personally. I'm sure there's a reason."

"I understand. Take care, Dr. Harkins."

"Please, call me Edward."

That brought a smile to the man's face.

"Edward. Thank you."

Harkins left, following the woman as she led him away, the entire time the floor moving and rolling. It was an odd sensation, one that suggested what it would've been like to maintain balance on a boat in water.

Soon, they arrived at an area that was completely different than the rest of the level. Where all of the walls were glass and see through, this section was made of grey walls and a stark brown door.

"Enter. Mr. Eldridge is already inside."

Harkins nodded and as she turned to leave he caught just a slight twitch in her neck. It was the first time he'd realized that she was animatronic.

5.

He entered to find Eldridge sitting in a chair in a room filled with computers and rows of ancient filing cabinets.

"Eldridge."

"Harkins"

"What's the meaning of all of this?" Harkins asked, looking around the room.

Eldridge remained sitting, licking his lips before motioning for Harkins to have a seat in the second chair.

"I've always considered you like a brother, Harkins. But when people start to ask questions and stick their noses somewhere they don't belong, it gets my hackles up."

"I'm sorry, Albert. I don't follow."

"Why did you want to see the machine that made the orbs?"

Harkins stuttered and stammered, surprised by the venom in Eldridge's voice.

"I've long been curious by the selection group and Salvation, Albert. We've talked about this. How could I, possessing such a highly attuned scientific mind, not be curious about the orbs?"

Harkins had seen Eldridge angry over their many years of friendship, but when Albert stood up and jabbed his right index finger into Harkins chest, he was shocked. The man was livid.

"How dare you think outside of your scope? You've grown too big for your station it seems. To think, I'd believed you to be trustworthy and a man who'd have my back."

"Wha... Huh? Where is this coming from, Eldridge? I was merely curious as to what the original device looked like when you made the first orb. I've always been loyal."

"That's not what Morton says," Eldridge said, interrupting.

"Excuse me? I've worked closely with Dr. Morton on her research. I've put aside my own work to help her with her mapping project."

"See. Bitter. Her work is ahead of yours. You can't handle that a woman has taken precedent over you, a man."

"I beg your pardon? I don't understand where your vitriol is coming from Albert, but I can assure you my interest was purely out of curiosity and nothing more."

He stood to leave, pushing Eldridge's hand away and stepping around the man, when Eldridge shoved him hard from behind. He fell forward and slammed into the closed door.

"What has come over you? Look at you," Harkins said, close to yelling. Eldridge was breathing heavy, teeth bared as though he was turning into an animal.

"Eldridge. It's me. Harkins. I'm here to be the best scientist I can. To make this ship the new earth. You know my loyalties lie with doing what's best. Let's just calm down and let cooler heads prevail."

It appeared as though the words had made their way into the Eldridge Harkins he knew. His body grew less tense, mouth closing, stepping back from the man.

"Fine. Go. But just know. I'm watching you."

Harkins hurriedly opened the door to leave, finding the woman waiting for him.

"Did Mr. Eldridge show you the origins of the orbs?" she asked, beginning to lead Harkins through the labyrinth of intelligent hallways.

"I'm afraid he did."

6.

Every part of Harkins told him to confront Morton. He didn't care if she was integral to the research or that Eldridge appeared to have a thing for her. She'd betrayed the trust he thought they had and was spreading misinformation to Eldridge behind his back.

But he knew better than that.

His own research needed to be completed.

The only way that could happen was for her to be successful and the only way that would happen was with his mind involved.

He marched back to their lab, ignoring the smirk on her face, and began to set up the microscopes that had been already delivered.

It was time to get back to work.

7.

'If only we would've known.'

A phrase spoken time and time again.

For the children who were left behind it meant nothing.

For the adults who'd realized the truth as the ship had launched and they'd remained behind, each word was a dagger when collected into that sentence.

8.

Harkins worked in silence over the next six months, only giving the occasional grunt or noise to signify he'd heard Morton if she asked a question. He ran the equations, examined the cells, worked on how the data effected the samples. Routine. He wasn't onboard to socialize and pat each other's backs. He was here to find the magic elixir that would allow the humans to return to the surface and call it home once again.

They were close, he knew it.

Then, one fateful morning, *that* sample arrived.

Blood had been drawn from the students who had been selected for Salvation. And while it wasn't known where they went when they caught their futures in the orbs that launched from below, they did leave behind plenty of samples for the scientists to examine and seek the hidden molecules that could counter the earth's changes.

"Where did this come from?" Harkins had asked in shock once he'd magnified the sample before him.

Morton took a look, her eyes growing wide.

She rushed to her work station bringing up the associated data.

"Here it is. This wasn't from a selected group," she said, herself surprised.

"Well, from where then?"
"Here, on the ship. This came from a young Ward."
Both looked at each other, not believing the news.
Harkins and Morton would need to make a visit.
He'd never been to the Ward Level before.

9.

"We'll stop here for the day," Harkins said, clapping his hands. The sound echoed in the confined classroom space.

He left the empty space behind, shuffling towards the exit. The sky had grown cloudy once again, the threat of a storm apparent.

Leaving the former school, he made his way through the empty streets of the small town. With every step he spared a glance towards the sky, looking to see if the storm clouds had arrived above. He hated looking up, knowing that the damned ship was above him somewhere.

Harkins spotted his house ahead at the top of the short hill.

Home.

It shouldn't give him any enjoyment or fill him with any feeling that wasn't despair, but every time he'd see it on the return trip his stomach would flutter as though reuniting with a relative he was fond of.

Entering the house he heard the patter of the rain hitting the roofing.

Just in time, he thought. He went and settled on the dusty recliner in the living room. He'd spend another night staring at the blank TV screen, imagining better days aboard a ship where he was respected.

He hoped the morning would bring sun.

10. GREY

Harkins started walking far before the morning light arrived.

When he'd first arrived on the planet, he'd been given some supplies ("I'm not a monster," Eldridge had said), but when those started to run low, panic began to set in.

The first house he'd stayed in was in shambles long before the world ended. It hadn't taken him long to realize that while the bombs had went off and wiped out most of the life on Earth, the blasts and radiation hadn't travelled as extensively as they'd been led to believe.

Another of Eldridge's deceptions.

Taking his time, he spent the next few weeks scouting houses until he found his current residence. Whomever had called this place home previously had been somebody who enjoyed knowledge. Harkins knew that from the moment he began taking inventory of what was in the house.

Three globes.

Two distinct sets of Encyclopedia's.

In the living room and both bedrooms, large maps of the Earth were tacked to the wall.

Perfect.

Harkins was even more pleased to find a map with a blown up section showing exactly where he was in the world. A remarkable stroke of luck, but considering everything that had occurred up until now, he was deserving of something good to come along.

So it was, that with the aid of the map, Harkins started to explore the world around him. Everything was new, exciting and scary. Surprisingly he found enough remnants of supplies and with the knowledge within the house, he was able to grow some food.

As the years passed, Harkins became comfortable with his existence, if not developing a bitterness towards Empyrean that simmered and needed to be frequently pushed down.

After much introspection, he decided that it was time to push his comfort zone a bit.

He saw that a city of considerable size was a mere ten miles to the North. Doing some rough math, Harkins believed it would take him around four hours to walk from the small town to the city.

His first trip would take the longest as he was unfamiliar with the area. Once he made it to the city, he would also need to spend considerable time searching for anything resembling supplies that he'd need. After; another four hours return trip.

He didn't feel totally comfortable attempting an overnight stay, but it very well might come down to that.

While walking to the city, which he dubbed 'Grey' due to the sheer amount of cement and buildings, he often thought back to that first visit. Ignorance and innocence were what led him to walk down the cracked and broken pavement, until he arrived at the outskirts. If he'd have been more 'world weathered' he may have been more on guard or attuned to arriving as a new comer to a place that time and people in power had long since forgotten about.

Hell, he chuckled, he still had the Empyrean Insignia on his left breast, the proud pin having once been personally clipped in place by Eldridge himself.

Eldridge.

That charlatan.

He'd also claimed that the Earth had reclaimed the surface. That buildings and roads had re-terraformed. As Harkins walked along the cracked cement he marvelled at just how wrong the man had been. Or deceptive. Which was more likely.

On his first trip to Grey, Harkins had brought an old bag and a pack with him, hoping to find enough supplies to keep him going for a few more weeks.

The conveniences of life on the ship were no longer here, no longer possible. There was no power grid, no electricity. But, Harkins did discover a generator. Fuel. It worked, much to his surprise.

How long had it been since the end of the world?

Harkins couldn't say with any confidence. It was a matter of Eldridge again concealing the data, hiding the information from the citizens. Some would say centuries. Others decades. Eldridge himself appeared to be a man who aged at an inhuman rate. Harkins remembered him visiting his own classroom when he first attended school on the revolving ship as a young boy. Harkins has been born on the ship that he was certain of. As for how long the ship had been orbiting the planet? Harkins wouldn't be able to hazard a guess. What he saw on the surface didn't compute. Decay and rot were occurring, this was certain *and* visible, but the Earth itself hadn't reclaimed what the humans had built. At least not here.

It was at the apex of a long hill that Harkins caught his first glimpse of Grey. He was stunned with what sprawled out ahead of him. An abandoned utopia of modernist architecture and feverish adulation towards Eldridge himself.

Harkins walked into the city along the crumbling remains of a freeway, passing under the curvature of an immense archway. He presumed the city's prior name had been carved into the archway, but the years had been equally unkind to the stone, the words long since fallen away and crushed on the roadway below.

Entering into the space, Harkins realized he was at a loss for words. The buildings that crowded each street were large, tall and barren. Some levels completely bare, save for the occasional root system or tree that'd grown within. At evenly spaced intervals, formerly magnificent statues and carvings were found. Cement and marble faces stared out into the distance no matter where Harkins looked. Each one paying tribute to Eldridge, Empyrean and the former government figures that'd at one time deemed themselves to resemble a God enough to have a master carver work the raw material into a piece of art.

The man was equal parts furious and equal parts ashamed. That he'd ever considered Eldridge a peer, something resembling a brother was ridiculous now, as he considered the apocalyptic museum of forgotten heroes.

As he continued down the main thoroughfare, Harkins was confident he'd end up at the City Center and if Eldridge's ego was as predictable as expected, there he'd find some sort of monument to himself and his ship.

11.

"And on this glorious morning, we give thanks to those who've stayed behind to see what will become of our planet."

Applause.

Tears.

"Detonation in 3...2...1..."

The movie theatre sized screen before Eldridge and the other Royals gathered showed the rockets at the height of their ascent.

Eldridge flipped the safety glass back, pushing the red button.

All of their eyes widened and grins spread across their faces as the image on the screen shared the mass explosions above the surface of the world.

12.

It wasn't until some months into Harkins banishment from the revolving ship that he realized two things. The first was that he had never been happier. The second was that he absolutely loved the walks to Grey.

Neither should've been plausible. He had been one of the brightest scientists on the revolving ship, a sterling accomplishment in its own right. As well, he'd needed a cane for some time now, ever since the incident.

He didn't think back on it often, but as he made his way down the dark and lonely highway towards Grey, his only companions were his own thoughts and the one-two-three sounds of each foot and his cane hitting the pavement.

When they'd discovered the sample and that the provider was currently residing on the Ward Level, Harkins had been over the moon. They put in the necessary paperwork to go meet with the child. They needed to decide on next steps and for what purposes they'd synthesize the sample.

Once they'd been cleared, they visited the Ward Level and Harkins was enamored with the child. They'd been living there since being abandoned in the Labor Level from a mother who'd had an unofficial pregnancy. Harkins, himself, had never been too fond of children, but talking to this little one was a breath of fresh air.

But what truly surprised him was how Morton responded. She hugged the child, fixed their hair, kept one arm around their shoulder.

He'd never seen this side of the woman.

On the elevator ride after, she was smiling the entire time.

"I'm going to adopt that child," she finally said.

"The hell you are."

"I will. You'll see."

Harkins watched Morton walk briskly away, the idea that she wanted to adopt and potentially sabotage the work infuriated him.

He didn't think anything more of it over the next few days as he continued assessing the sample and watching its properties that he found absolutely fascinating.

When a man entered the lab and told him Eldridge had requested a meeting, he was surprised. He followed the man, unsure what was happening.

They rode the elevator in silence.

When it continued travelling up, it dawned on Harkins that they weren't stopping at the Meeting Level.

"Where are we going?"

"Mr. Eldridge has requested you visit him on his own level."

Harkins felt unease growing. He grew sweaty.

Why did Eldridge want to meet here?

When the doors opened onto the Level, Harkins was overcome with awe. Eldridge had spared no expense on his personal living level. Fountains greeted the two as they left the elevator. Harkins saw what appeared to be dogs scampering about in an open grass field, he shook his head. He'd long believed no animals had been brought onto the ship when it left Earth. An impressive mansion sat beyond two ponds, a gold plated pathway leading up to the stairs.

Eldridge himself sat on the steps, with what looked to be a bottle of beer in one hand. Another thing Harkins had learned about but didn't know survived.

It was all adding up for Harkins. That Eldridge wasn't as forthcoming with everything as he'd believed and a part of him was hurt that he'd never been to this place before, what with they're long friendship. That hurt was amplified ten-fold when Morton appeared from inside, also carrying a bottle of beer.

"Ah, Harkins. Glad you could join us. We have some *things* to discuss."

"Is that beer? Look, I don't have time to be pulled away from the research. Morton, have you told him about the advancements we've made in cellular regrowth just these last few days?"

"I have."

"So, you two both know how important it is for me to get back down to the lab and continue."

"There's a reason you're here, Harkins," Eldridge said, the tone in his voice taking a dark turn. "The cellular regrowth is directly related to that."

"What do you mean?" he asked, thrown off when two guards came and stood beside him.

"Morton here tells me you were mocking her when she suggested she adopt. Harkins..." He let out a long sigh, frustration boiling over at something Harkins didn't understand. "Look, you're supposed to help Morton. From what she's told me and relayed time and time again, you just can't seem to let it go that she's onto something immense. I've had enough."

Harkins went to object when the two guards grabbed him, each taking one of his arms. Eldridge waved a hand and before Harkins knew what was happening, one of the guards threw him to the ground, the other producing a machete.

"Take off the left leg."

Eldridge and Morton turned and went into the mansion, the door closing as the guard swung as hard as they could.

13.

Harkins woke gripped in the sweaty hallucinations of a fever dream. He thrashed his body and gasped for air as a nurse hustled over and gave him a sedative.

He did notice that he had both legs as he drifted back into unconsciousness.

14.

In the weeks and months that followed, Harkins pushed his anger and bitterness to the side. He wanted to heal, needed to become whole again and if what Morton and he had been working on in the lab, regarding cell regeneration was correct, he knew his leg would repair itself and this damn cane would be tossed aside.

Morton wouldn't speak to him aside from clinical questions. Eldridge was off limits, Harkins told as much when he regained consciousness.

He was now confined to a research medical room, on the Medical Level, himself now a test subject. He asked Morton several times if he could see the data, look at samples of his tissue in the microscopes, but was rebuffed every time.

His brilliant mind became his prison as much as the four walls and locked door. Harkins longed to know the progress of his research. Of how his leg was doing and where he was falling on the spectrum of acceptable parameters versus his cells dying and his prognosis poor.

Long hours spent reflecting on how he'd ended up here always brought him back to a single thought. Her. Morton.

He'd had no issues prior to that meeting so many moons ago with Eldridge and her. She had it out for him, for some reason.

She had Eldridge in her right hand and was looking to adopt the child in the Ward and synthesize their blood for her own purposes. Most likely for Eldridge.

Wishing he knew a way to undo what'd been done, Harkins decided his best course of action was to remain patient, silent and diligent. He'd strike when the iron was hot.

15.

*

The two children held hands as they walked through the darkened streets.

Above them the revolving ship hung like a glow-in-the-dark star stuck to the roof of a child's room.

The air was blistering hot, the dust stinging their eyes, but that was no matter.

Arriving at the former Town Hall, they laid the required offering of coins at the feet of the effigy to the Empyrean ruler. Hoping that this weeks collection would be enough to appease the tyrant and he'd provide them with food and medicine.

*

16.

When Harkins arrived at the City Center for the first time, he fell to his knees, wincing with pain. Pain from his injury, pain from his age and the distance of the walk. But also pain for the people who'd been sacrificed for Eldridge's ego and desire to be recognized and revered as a God.

"I know we must leave family and friends behind. This is a hard reality. To those who remain behind, we shall never forget you. We will meet again.

Harkins began to cry as he read the words carved into the plaque that sat at the base of Eldridge's shrine.

A raised base of bronze, thirty feet by thirty feet, making a square that took up the center of the space. On the base were bronze statues that featured some dogs playing, kids cavorting and near the middle the revolving ship which was attached to the booster rocket that allowed it to lift off from the surface and launch into space. Harkins immediately recognized the statue that was Eldridge. The man was smiling, one hand on the back of a woman, her baby the focus of their attention.

He wanted to puke. To find something to bash this spectacle to pieces and destroy the lies that it stood for. Everything showcased on that base, except for Eldridge himself, had been eradicated and vaporized when Eldridge had flipped that switch and ignited those warheads.

As he went to stand, somebody took him by the arm, helping him to his feet. Harkins shuddered in shock and turned, preparing to be attacked by some unseen assailant.

Instead, he found himself looking at a face he'd not seen in decades. A face from someone he'd thought had long ago passed away.

"Harkins? It is you," the man said, pulling him in and hugging him.

Once they'd stepped apart, Harkins looked at the man, seeing his face blistered and bandages placed haphazardly to protect other parts of his bald head.

"Thompson. I can't believe my eyes. You're still alive? How? What... how?"

Thompson laughed, the sound music to Harkins ears.

"Come, old friend. I'll make us some tea and we can catch up."

Harkins agreed and followed his old friend, wondering just what had happened to have had him end up here and not jettisoned as he'd thought.

17. Thompson

They walked through the silent streets of a city decaying and slowly being reclaimed by the weeds and grass.

Harkins found it unsettling that no lights were on. No sound of any kind other than the noise of their feet hitting the ground.

The sun had travelled far across the sky from when he'd arrived. With the scope of the buildings around them, the light was blocked and the air was chilled. A slight wind whipped up and spilled through the openings, an unseen river being pushed by the buildings. As it increased in strength, random pieces of discarded material clattered and banged, Harkins finding that he was on edge and nervous.

"Nothing to fear, here," Thompson said, sensing Harkins response. "I'll introduce you to some others shortly, but for now, just know you're safe."

Harkins nodded, not completely sure he trusted what Thompson said.

"How's the leg doing? Knee injury?"

"Bit more than that."

"From when you landed?"

"No. From Eldridge."

"What? Really?"

"Yes, 'fraid so. Seems we have some catching up to do."

Thompson chuckled.

Even in the dimming light, Harkins could see the various statues and faded murals as they weaved through the streets. Stone shrines to lions, bears, tigers and other large animals decorated the corners and edges of buildings. It was the sculptures of the men that were most unsettling to Harkins. It was as though they'd been frozen in time, covered in bronze and left to spend eternity on a planet that had been abandoned. He wondered if the soul of those immortalized still resided within. If he knelt before them and listened close, would he hear them whisper?

"Almost there. You need a break?"

"No, thank you though."

"You sure? You're slowing?"

"Am I? Apologies. Lost in thought."

The wind changed direction and turned towards the two men, the force enough to cause them both to stagger and step closer to the nearest building. Harkins leaned against the bronze likeness of a horse, while Thompson stood beside Harkins.

"Harkins, you alright? That's quite the smile."

He hadn't even realized he was smiling, but he was.

"I am. It's just... it's hard to describe, but it's a smell. Do you smell that?"

"I do."

"What is that?" Harkins asked

"BBQ. It's near dinnertime."

"It smells glorious."

The two started off again, now that the wind had lessoned. Rounding the corner, Thompson let out a loud whistle.

A whistle replied and Thompson waved.

On the top floor of the apartment building before them, Harkins spotted two figures waving back, standing on the balcony.

"We're here. Are you hungry?"

"That I am."

Thompson led Harkins into a darkened lobby of the building. It took them another twenty minutes of looping around and around up the stairs to reach the top floor. Once there, Thompson pushed open the door and led them down the hallway to an open apartment door.

Inside were two men.

18.

Thompson ushered Harkins inside, closing the door and sliding a wooden plank down to ensure it remained closed.

Harkins noted this, confused after Thompson had expressed their safety earlier.

"Harkins, this is Percival and Rajminder."

They both gave smiled at Harkins but neither felt genuine.

He nodded back, wondering about the marks that peppered both of their faces.

Thompson himself was in the process of unwrapping his own bandages. Once done, he set them in a pot and filled it with water, before turning on the stove to bring it to a boil.

"You have power?"

"Sparingly. We have funnelled most of the natural gas to our apartment here. Raj has an engineering background. He was able to get things sorted. Really, those two are responsible for our 'conveniences.'"

In the low light, Harkins could see the glistening wounds that pocked Thompson's scalp. He wanted to ask but didn't want to overstep, having just arrived.

"If you're wondering about my wounds, or the marks on those two, just ask. We have nothing to hide," he replied, as though reading his mind.

"I am, actually. But, if it's all the same, later? I'd love to know more about this place down here."

Raj chuckled, moved to sit on the couch. Percival remained standing, his body position worried Harkins. He'd seen that stance a number of times in his life, usually right before an act of violence happened.

"You Eldridge scum?" Percival finally said, shifting his weight back and forth on his feet. Harkins watched as he opened and closed his hands, the knuckles growing white each time.

"Easy, Perc. Harkins is a good man, I knew him when I was on the ship."

"Did you now? That was how many years ago? That fucker Eldridge left people down here. Left them to die. Now, what? He just shows up?"

"Were you left behind?" Harkins asked, taking a half step back, putting some distance between them.

"Nah. My grandparents were though."

"Fascinating."

"Fascinating?" Harkins didn't have time to react to the anger. He was so far in his own mind trying to calculate numbers and determine the differences between time moving from the Earth to the ship that he only realized what was happening after Percival had punched him. He dropped hard to the floor from the first right hand to the chin, legs going wobbly and no longer able to support him. He was mildly aware of Raj and Thompson telling Percival to stop and grabbing at the man above him, even as Percival managed to strike Harkins three more times with solid punches to the head.

When Percival was pulled off, Harkins pushed himself to a sitting position, licking the blood from where one of his lips had been busted open. He eyed the man, but found he wasn't angry. He was still running numbers through his head and everything was slotting into place.

"Fascinating," he mumbled to himself, standing. He found his cane and went to the deck, looking out into darkness that now claimed the night sky.

"Harkins, you ok?"

Thompson joined him on the deck.

Looking inside, Harkins saw Raj sitting beside Percival on the couch, the two in animated conversation.

"I am. Thank you. I should've chosen a better word, I think." He offered a smile, his lip swollen.

"Maybe, but that was unacceptable. Percival knows better than to react like that."

"Why do you barricade the door?" Harkins asked, motioning towards the entrance.

"We barricade the door for our safety from being raided. We never really know when any Returners have been deployed. Or the tall one that watches. They're all ruthless and won't hesitate to kill if we offer any resistance."

"The Returners? No. Surely, that's incorrect. The group is for dedicated scientific research. Surface exploration and reclamation advances."

Thompson laughed, shaking his head at Harkins obvious lack of understanding.

"Harkins, has anything you've seen here on the surface thus far matched up with Eldridge or the Returners reports? When I was exiled, I was under the assumption that Earth had been reclaimed by the surface. Buildings grown over. Animals long since extinct. That the people who stayed had long ago died. Look around, you're smart. Connect the dots."

He had been actively analyzing everything since the day he'd landed.

"Thompson. The reason I said 'fascinating' was because of the numbers I'm running in my head. The difference between time on the ship and time on the surface. Eldridge has figured out a way to modify time on the ship. It must be based around the revolutions as well as the number of times it travels around the planet. It's fascinating."

"It is. I'm nowhere near as smart as yourself, but I've been trying to figure that out since my arrival. When I was on the ship, I had been led to believe it had been a few thousand years since we'd left the surface. But down here it's only been a hundred or so years."

"I must admit, when I travelled here to the city, I was looking for some supplies and was planning on returning. But running into you has changed that. May I spend the night and mull over how to use this information?"

"Use this information?"

"I need to get back on the ship. I need to kill Eldridge."

"Ah," replied Thompson. "Well that we agree on."

19.

They didn't speak much more that night.

Harkins sat in a chair watching the stars and every so often he'd catch a light turning on and off in buildings around them.

There are others.

A thought he struggled to fathom as he attempted to correlate every new piece of information he'd ingested.

As he drifted off to sleep in the lumpy chair, he realized he missed the bed back in the small town, something he'd never have believed before.

The morning brought low clouds and with them, ominous thoughts.

Harkins didn't like how Percival looked at him. He stayed near the couch with Raj, both talking and glancing at him frequently.

Thompson was the last to wake, Harkins feeling relieved when he made his way down the hallway, yawning and absently scratching an armpit.

"Apologies, Thompson. I know you've just woke up but I do need to find some supplies and make my way back. Could you point me in the right direction?"

Thompson, Raj and Percival all shared a look that Harkins didn't enjoy.

He moved towards the door, wanting to flee, not wanting to wait to be bound and tortured. The memory of what Eldridge's guards had done still fresh.

Thompson stepped between him and the door, his hands grabbing Harkins shoulders.

"Just hold up, Harkins. I swear we're not going to hurt you."

He released the man's shoulders before continuing.

"We want your help. We've discovered a few things here. If you'll accept my invitation, I'd love to have a chat with you. We can walk and gather some supplies together."

Harkins agreed, but only if it was the two of them.

He went and waited on the steps, watching the scene before him with a sense of surrealism.

In all of the old news videos and photos, streets like this were depicted as busy. Cars driving, people walking, the hustle and bustle of life spilling from sidewalk to roadway and back again.

Yet, here he sat.

Alone.

Not a car in sight, nor a person. For a solid fifteen minute stretch nothing even moved in any direction. It wasn't until Thompson came outside that the stillness was broken. Harkins found that the serene setting had been filling something within that he hadn't considered needing filled.

"Eerie, isn't it?" Thompson asked, when they started walking away from the building.

"Yes and no. I'm still a bit stunned that all of this exists. I believed that everything had been taken back by the wilderness."

"Me as well. When I first met Percival and Raj, I was shocked that they were relatives of those who had stayed behind. You know they'd been dubbed something? Those left behind."

"I did."

"They prefer to not be called that anymore. Feel it's derogatory."

"I can see that. It also puts a target on them."

"It sure does. Especially when Returners come."

"Can you tell me more about that? I'd been led to believe they were a scientific group who came here to study and track Earth's progress so we could live here again one day."

"From what I've learned, from a very reliable source, Returners are not so scientific. They mostly come to the surface every few weeks to steal any supplies we've managed to collect and on occasion they'll leave behind food for us. The main guy, an Eldridge relative if you can believe that, has a number of addictions, so if we can make him the stuff he needs, he'll often times boost what supplies he's delivering."

"But you all fear them?"

"They're not nice people, Harkins. They'll kill you if needed."

Harkins nodded, stopping for a moment to take in the architecture of the city around them. He should've been amazed by the gargoyles that looked down upon them and the statues that stood like sentinels everywhere he looked. Instead, he saw more pomp. More grandiosity that most likely took away from aid to the people who lived here.

"So, tell me, Harkins. What's with the limp?"

Harkins offered a smile, breathing out longer than he'd expected.

"Eldridge. Cut it off. Well, one of his guards."

21.

Morton continued to treat Harkins like a patient, any pretense of them having been colleagues once long gone.

He stopped asking questions, instead mentally cataloging everything. What she was doing, the methodology of her movements. He began to build an internal hypothesis over how the blood experiments had progressed. Harkins saw first-hand how the injections and topical administered formula were regenerating his damaged leg. The strength was slowly coming back.

Each day, a man came and forced him to walk laps around the confined space, a cane helping to balance him as he moved.

It was on one of those laps that he noticed Morton watching him through the window of the door to the room. Standing beside her was a young person.

"She did it," he said.

"You talking to me, Harkins?" the trainer/guard asked, shoulders rounding back in a posture he didn't appreciate.

"No, sorry. Just speaking aloud."

"Shut up and keep walking."

He kept his head down, only glancing at Morton's smirk as he made his way around that corner of the room.

He wished he could take in more details of the youngster beside Morton, but he knew in his heart that Morton had adopted the child from the Ward Level. She'd done it. Direct access to the source of their experiment. Or rather *her* experiment now.

*

"Why are we not going outside? I wanna sit on the grass," the boy said, face twisting into a pout.

"Mom said we can't. Something is falling from the sky. She say's it'll hurt us," the girl said, flopping onto the floor.

"I don't care. Mom doesn't know everything."

He went to the door, the girl standing quickly to protest but it was no use.

The door was flung open, the former world of color still drowned in the charcoal grey of ash. In the distance, fires burned, sirens sounded.

"When will this go away? Return to how it was?" he asked.

"Never," the kid's mom replied, walking to shut the door.

Outside, the acid rain increased in intensity, the world growing darker.

*

22.

"So, how did you go from walking around in circles in your room to down here?" Thompson asked.

Harkins was enjoying the walk, seeing the details of this place. It felt good to just *be* while walking with Thompson.

"I saw my chance and I took it."

23. Jettisoned

Harkins knew that the moment was right when Morton was bent down in front of him, testing the capillary refill of his foot. Harkins didn't hesitate, nor did he feel guilty, when in one smooth motion he grabbed her head and drove his knee into the side of her face as hard as he could. She let out a pained sound as she crumpled to the floor. Harkins waited half a second to make sure he saw her stomach rise and fall, he wanted to hurt her not kill her, before he made his exit from the room and began to move across the level towards the elevator as fast as he could.

Somehow he was able to avoid being seen, making it to the elevator. That was when he realized he was hooped.

He had no ID. No scan card. He couldn't access the elevator and if he found a way to access it, he wouldn't be able to enter any levels once there.

It was no matter.

While he stood analyzing the elevator before him and ran scenarios through his mind, the elevator itself opened and Eldridge stepped out, two guards flanking him.

"Harkins. You disappoint me. It pains me to think of how far you've fallen in such a short time."

He had no fight in him. He knew the laws, knew the repercussions for attacking Dr. Morton. The guards grabbed his arms and dragged him as they followed Eldridge.

Morton appeared, still rubbing her head, at the entrance to the Medical Examination Level.

"You get to decide," Eldridge said. "What do you want us to do with Harkins?"

Morton looked at Harkins. He wouldn't give her the satisfaction of seeing fear so he kept her gaze, wanting her to look away first.

While maintaining eye contact she spoke one word that broke Harkins resolve.

"Jettison."

Harkins wanted to beg and plead for his life, to protest and fight for why he shouldn't be thrown from the ship, why he did what he did, but it was no good. He knew Eldridge had been looking for a reason to kick him off. He'd cut one of his legs off already. And if, for some reason, Eldridge had a change or heart and let him stay, unrest within the citizens would grow. They'd question why someone broke the law, assaulted another, and was allowed to stay on board, when so many of their own family members had been jettisoned for acts far less than assault.

There was no going back.

The two guards picked Harkins up, carrying him between them.

Eldridge and Morton walked just behind the trio, talking rapidly but their voices too low for Harkins to hear. Unable to understand what they were saying didn't really matter, ultimately. Harkins had only seconds of life left.

It was then that he realized, where normal people would have all of their precious memories flash before their eyes, Harkins had none. His life had been and always was, dedicated to science and advancement.

A strange sorrow took hold. He had no family. Nothing that made staying on the ship that meaningful, when he truly assessed his situation.

So, when they arrived at the Jettison/Incinerator Level, he was calm and collected.

"Harkins," Eldridge said, as they stood before a jettison tube. "Morton and I spoke while we followed. I, nor her, believe you deserve to die. As you know, I am a most forgiving and humble man. I have decided to jettison you, but you will not die. God speed, old friend. How I wish things had turned out differently."

"Wait, what?" Harkins tried to ask, but Eldridge and Morton left, as the two guards shoved him into the vessel that would rocket out into space and eject him.

He began to wail, tears coming fast as the lid closed and the rocket accelerated, flying out into the open blackness.

24.

"But it came here," Thompson said.

"It did."

*

Harkins kept his eyes tightly closed and held his breath for as long as possible. He knew that once the lid popped and the seat ejected him, he'd be ejected out into the vast vacuum of space, his insides sucked out through the openings in his body. He almost wished they'd incinerated him first before jettisoning his ashes. At least a pod wouldn't have been wasted on him.

But...

Absence of sound.

Absence of pressure.

Absence of cold.

A chime sounded.

He opened his eyes, stunned to find the vessel was travelling towards the planet, shocked to find no timer displaying how long until ejection.

"Harkins, I know you can hear me," Eldridge's voice sounded through the speaker system.

Can he see me?

"Ed, Edward. We've been friends since you were little. Hell, I thought at one point you'd take over my position should I pass away. But life has conspired to send us down different paths. Mainly, you've thrown away your academia and are now forbidden from the ship. As a humble man, I have forgiven you. I couldn't bring myself to jettison you, so I'm sending you to the surface where you can live out however long you have left of your life. I've included some supplies – I'm not a monster – to see you through the first bit of your time down there. After that... you're on your own. Godspeed, old friend."

The coms went silent, the ship ticking and clicking as the outside pressures of space pushed against the body of the vessel.

Harkins looked at the planet as it approached, wondering just how long he had left to live.

If he could find a way to make Eldridge pay he would, but a part of him realized that may be an impossibility.

25.

"And here I am."

"Here you are. Funny you say about getting revenge on Eldridge. That's how we all feel. And I think we have something that you may be able to help us with."

"Oh?"

"Come, I'll show you."

His curiosity was piqued, as they began to move further through 'Grey.' It was an interesting mix of buildings known as skyscrapers as well as shorter, business frontages. Harkins felt dismay over the darkness within all of them, knowing at one point this area would have been a bustling place filled with people.

"This way," Thompson said, as they made a left and entered a different section of the town.

"What is this area? It is very different."

"This used to be labelled an Industrial Complex. The spaces were reserved for manufacturing based businesses."

It made sense to Harkins, seeing the change in building design and the fences and rusted machines that filled the lots.

"Come, here, this way," Thompson said, his voice bursting with energy now.

He was jogging ahead of Harkins now, who struggled to keep up. His leg was the strongest it had been since before it'd been cut off, but it still had its limitations. Thompson waited for him, at the entrance to a large bay door.

"We found this on a scavenging trip. We initially weren't sure what it was, but then after I found some boxes filled with old manuals, I stumbled on what it is."

He grabbed a chain near the ground and pulled, the door loudly clattering open.

The space within was dark, Harkins waited until Thompson flipped a large switch and the interior illuminated.

"Solar power. Still works!"

Thompson disappeared into the building, Harkins close behind. The area directly inside was an open bay, with work stations set up along the right side. Turning to the left, Harkins came to a stop, mouth hanging open.

"It can't be..." he finally said, voice trembling.

"It is!"

He took a few steps towards the immense bay on the left, his hand reaching out. If he could've thrown his cane away and sprinted he would've.

Before Harkins sat the original orb machine. He knew it the moment he saw it. An impressive device that looked very similar to an oversized microscope, he made a long loop around the contraption, taking it all in.

"Eldridge refused to show me when I asked."

"That's because he couldn't show you."

"This is beautiful. Just... beautiful," he said, letting his hand fall onto the surface of the machine. His eyes followed the tubing that extended from an area with a small door, up the tubes and all the way to the launcher. He looked at the chair were the operator would sit, sighting the launch line and pressing the button that would propel the orb far up into the atmosphere. It would travel up and up and up until one of the students selected for Salvation would grab it and find their future.

"Did the manual show how it worked?"

Thompson held up a finger, knelt beside the device where Harkins couldn't see and following a noise, stood and smiled as the device hummed and came to life.

"You can still turn it on?" Harkins was elated.

"But what does this have to do with revenge on Eldridge?" he finally asked, still looking over the framework.

"The orbs are currently being produced and launched at a facility near a lake. They have people who man the place, but they rotate out every eight hours and have a crew who work there when it's Salvation time. Through reconnaissance we've come up with a plan. We take over the station, replace the material the orbs are being made out of and exact some revenge."

Thompson was smiling with glee while sharing their plans.

"How're we going to get this machine from here to there?"

"We don't need to. They have an identical one already in the silo. But this allows us to practice. We just don't understand completely how it works. That's where you come in."

"I see," he said. He was playing what Thompson said over and over in his mind. *Would it work? Could they do it? Could he do it?* He suspected it was probable. The machine wasn't overly complicated. Something else clicked while he was examining the hatch and spotted a discolored section on the outer shell.

"Does this plan have anything to do with your bandages?"

"It does. You see, we want to fill the orbs with *something* that'll burn up the chosen jumpers. We've been experimenting with different materials. Hence the bandages."

"Well, I guess if we want to make this happen, I should expect to be burned," Harkins said with a laugh.

26.

*

Someone joins the child. They are running, jumping, laughing and throwing sand along with them. The child looks, seeing a beautiful woman. Long black hair, dark eyes, a smile that warms their heart. They leap into the woman's arms, the hug a moment of predestined euphoria that sends a message from child to adult and back again.

We are whole, it says. We are meant to be one. Together.

The woman kneels, letting go of the child. She smiles, the child reciprocates. It's only then that they spot the insignia of the Higher Levels on the woman's shirt.

The two adults have now arrived, both giving the child a lecture on respecting royalty and acting appropriately.

"Enough," the woman says, shutting them both up instantly.

"Lizzie, would you like to come live with me?"

"Yes, please."

She stands, taking the child's hand.

The two walk away from the adults, aware of the man walking with them, but not paying him mind.

Lizzie leaves the Ward Level, never to return.

*

27. Progress

Thompson accompanied Harkins back to his home. The two shared a laugh at the coincidence that Eldridge had abandoned Harkins in the quaint town that housed the orb machine.

The two friends sat on the dock overlooking the water before Thompson returned to 'Grey.' They spoke of things friends speak of who've not seen each other in years.

A perfect day filled with sun, warmth of companionship and the desire of a common goal.

Harkins would begin some initial experiments shortly, first wanting to study the manual of the machine before really diving into it.

That evening, Thompson bid farewell. He'd be returning with Percival and Raj in a month's time, the trio ready to join Harkins in preparation to storm the silo and take control of the device within.

Not long after midnight, many hours after Thompson had left, Harkins stood in the kitchen of his home, enjoying the familiarity of the structure. He hadn't lived there long, but it felt like *his* already. Staring through the window towards the night sky, he wondered if Eldridge was looking down upon the planet he left behind. He expected not, but a part of him hoped he was, hoped he could sense the anger he was directing towards the ship and towards the man who'd exiled him not long ago.

28.

Two weeks.

For two weeks, Harkins worked himself to the bone. He got up earlier each day, reading the manual, drawing schematics and hypothesizing different concoctions. He went to bed later and later with numbers and chemical equations dancing behind closed eyes.

On the first day of week three, Harkins decided he needed a break. To let his brain rest. So, he went for a walk, wishing to explore the small town more than he'd done thus far.

He shuffled along, down one street and onto the next. Walked by boarded up shops, overgrown houses, forgotten cars. Where Empyrean had fed them the lie that the surface had reclaimed everything, Harkins saw that in some cases they'd been close to the truth. Weathered leather eaten away in the interiors of the vehicles, roots having grown up and through businesses and buildings.

It was on one such turn that Harkins discovered the school across the empty parking lot. He'd never seen such a haunted place before in his life, the echoes of long-gone students rattled around his head as he approached the front door.

With some effort he pushed the door open, the hinges squealing and groaning. The hallway that stretched out was dimly illuminated from light that spilled in from the windows of each classroom.

He proceeded with a heavy heart. Knowledge had always been his passion. To see this place in such a state of disrepair hurt. Eldridge had let all these children down. Just like all the children selected for Eradication. A mad man. Harkins would've spit on the floor if not for the respect he had for what this place used to be.

He stepped tentatively into the first classroom, finding the empty desks pointed to the teacher's desk at the front. He went and stood behind it, tapping his cane against the wood as though calling the class to attention.

"Good morning class," he said, with no hint of foolishness. He smiled, thinking of the faces that should've been looking back at him, that should've been sitting in this room, ready and eager to learn.

"My name is Dr. Harkins. Ed to my friends. Let's open our books and begin, shall we."

For the next several hours, Harkins gave an imaginary lesson to some make believe students. By the end of the morning, he could picture each student completely in their assigned desks. He felt the pangs of ache again over the situation, longing to see the blank spots fill in with real kids, but that would never happen.

When he felt like he was done, he clapped his hands, promised to return to the lesson the following day, said his goodbyes and left the school. He'd originally planned on returning to the beach but not anymore. He was going to sit on the dock, enjoy the cool breeze that offset the warmth of the sun, but after his stint as teacher to the ghosts of the town he needed to go home.

Decompress.

29.

Harkins had visited the school each morning for the next week.

In the afternoons he began to search through the science lab just down the hall. Accessing the chemicals that were stored in the former teacher's room, he started experimenting. He worked on a concoction that he believed would be a viable option to be infused each orb.

Refining the solution meant he soon joined Thompson, Raj and Percival by having to bandage his head. By the end of the week, he decided to cut off his hair, making it easier to treat the sores and wrap the bandages tighter and around his head.

As the sun set on another day, Harkins realized he'd zoned out. He'd not been wanting to admit it, but lately his memory had been fading. Trouble remembering words or phrases and at times he'd day dreamed longer than normal. Even the understanding of time had become difficult. He thought he knew how long he'd been on the surface, but he was anything but confident about it.

Maybe it was his body adjusting to being down here versus up there, but everything was foggy and difficult when he tried to focus.

He shook his head, trying to get his eyes to stop being blurry when he spotted motion outside the school. At first his brain suggested it was students playing after the last bell, but reality returned. There were no kids within twenty miles of this town. He knew that.

Instead, he watched as soldiers wearing Empyrean suits ran in formation. They had packs on and carried the standard energy stun-guns. Their helmets had dark face shields which didn't allow Harkins to see through, but once he figured out who they were his heart sank.

They were Returners.

They were looking for him.

*

The first raids happened one month after the bombs exploded.

The Inhabitors had remained inside, sheltering from the initial fallout and providing medical attention to those family members who suffered burns and wounds.

No warning was given, no announcements made.

Doors began to be battered, broken down and Returners entered without calling out a single word. Those who resisted were electrocuted or beaten to death. Those who stayed silent lived and helped to gather some of their supplies so the Empyrean soldiers could transport them back to the ship.

'For the good of the Royals,' they'd tell the Inhabitors as the loaded up whatever was gathered.

The farmers who'd been left behind to grow crops in mass quantities, fared no better. Returners took their children in some cases. In other cases, if supplies weren't up to expectations the farms were burned to the ground.

They'd leave, lives destroyed, rations diminished.

But the Inhabitors lived as best they could, with one thought always at the front of their minds.

They'll be back.

The Returners would always come back.

*

31.

Harkins fled from the lab, stumbled over a discarded chair before regaining his feet and moved as fast as he could towards the far end of the darkened hallway. He pushed through the double doors once there, entering the cavernous gymnasium. He'd never set foot in this place since discovering the school. He wasn't sure why. He'd opened the doors and stared inside, but something had prevented him from ever entering. Maybe it was his wish to not disturb the memories of previous games played, the student's celebrations frozen in time. Or maybe it was the depth of the blackness that lined the perimeter at the far side, his fear of the unknown still fresh no matter how long he'd lived on this planet.

For whatever reason, he hadn't. But now it was necessary and for a brief moment Harkins realized this may be the last place he'd ever see.

Finding a storage space tucked away behind bleachers that were halfway pushed back against the wall, he squeezed himself into the dark spot and waited.

Every creak, groan and crack that sounded in the dark gym made him flinch and hold his breath. His thoughts turned to Thompson, Raj and Percival. All three would've been on their way to the town. They were going to do their reconnaissance and plan out how to take possession of the silo. Something clicked for Harkins. The arrival of the Returners was all too convenient.

Against better judgement he wiggled free before tentatively approaching the entrance to the gym. Finding the hallway clear, he ducked from the gym into the classroom directly to the right, wanting to get a good view of the courtyard and playground. Once he cleared some dirt and dust from the window, he was able to see out.

Thompson stood with another soldier, one who he recognized immediately as Jack Eldridge. Raj and Percival were blindfolded and on their knees before the two men, a dozen soldiers surrounding them.

It had been a set up.

Before Harkins could even formulate another angry thought, Eldridge stepped forward and jabbed his stun gun to the side of Percival's head. The man's body went rigid and shuddered, smoke puffing from where the device was pressing against the skin. Eldridge pulled the gun away, then kicked the deceased's body over. He turned and repeated the process with Raj. Harkins should've yelled, should've distracted them in the hopes that maybe Raj would survive, but he didn't. He didn't want to be discovered. Thompson would be looking for him now, he needed to hide again, even if it felt hopeless.

The front doors of the school clanged open.

Harkins rushed to the entrance of the classroom, hoping his leg would handle the stress. He peeked around the doorframe, seeing two soldiers enter each of the far classrooms. Knowing this was his chance, he escaped back into the gym, returning to the storage space. He pulled his cane in behind him as he heard the doors to the gym slam against the walls as soldiers made their way inside.

Lights beamed from where they were attached to the stun guns, illuminating parts of the darkened gym. Harkins forced himself to remain still, to slow his breathing and ignore the tiny voice in the back of his mind that told him he was going to be killed.

The footsteps grew nearer as the lights flashed left to right as they swept the room. He pulled tight, trying to forcefully shrink his body. The backside of an impossibly tall soldier stepped into view, blocking the entrance to the storage space. The soldier was less than a foot away. Harkins froze as the soldier's beam of light illuminated in front of them. Then, the figure moved away, their steps echoing as they returned to the entrance of the gym.

"All clear," Harkins heard someone say. More fading steps as the soldiers went down the hallway.

Harkins didn't move.

The doors of the school slammed shut.

Harkins didn't move.

How many soldiers had entered the school? The gym? He didn't know but he didn't want to risk leaving his hiding place too soon after believing he was safe to only find himself at the end of the electric stun guns. He'd remembered some of the feedback on the testing when they were developed all those years ago and knew he didn't want to be on the wrong end of one. His mind went to Percival and Raj, how they'd stood no chance against the current that had ripped through their brains.

Harkins remained there for hours. His legs cramped, he let himself piss where he lay huddled in the dark, but there he stayed until he was certain no soldier remained in the dark.

When he pulled himself free, everything stung and ached when he stood. He gave himself time to let his legs steady, his weak leg remaining numb during the first half dozen steps.

Making it to the gym entrance, he looked down the hallway, finding it empty. He shuffled over into the classroom, returning to where he watched them execute the two men. No soldiers. They'd taken the dead with them. He didn't know where they'd take the bodies, for all he knew they may just toss them in the lake, but for now, it appeared as thought the soldiers had left. Did that mean they'd also left the surface? Returned to the ship? Harkins had no idea, but he decided for now, he was going to spend the night in the school. He didn't want to risk stumbling upon soldiers on patrol. For all he knew, his adopted residence had been combed over and his meager belongings tossed around.

He made his way to the former nurse's room. Once inside, he closed the door and placed a chair against it, jamming it under the handle. A narrow sky light above let him see just enough of his surroundings to find the cot in the corner. Pulling the musty blanket over his body, Harkins let out a long sigh, the stress of the day washing away.

Sleep came easily that night, Harkins slipping off into dreamland within minutes.

32.

*

The world didn't end overnight.

Leaders of various governments had been monitoring changes over the course of hundreds of years. First it was changes due to Climate. Famine, floods, heat waves and wildfires. All linked back to mankind's impact on the planet. Polar ice began to melt, the oceans rising. First it was only a few inches. Then feet. The landmasses began to be rebuilt as the water claiming more of the shoreline. Soon entire cities were uninhabitable, the populations forced to relocate further inland.

Infrastructure couldn't handle the unexpected influx. Power grids became unpredictable, hospital systems overloaded.

Meanwhile, the Earth's population continued to grow, until leaders began to propose sterilization programs. Family size limits were put in place, as protests erupted and personal rights were infringed upon.

By then, it was already too late. The governments knew that habitation of the planet was failing, that a new plan needed to be sourced and sourced quickly. Without a sister planet to travel to, the next best possibility was the development and manufacturing of space stations. But like many things in the world, this had already been sabotaged by the powers that be. Empyrean had been secretly building a revolving ship, beginning when Australia and New Zealand had been flooded and disappeared from satellite imagery. When most of Europe and half of India had vanished from the rising ocean levels, Albert Eldridge had introduced the ship to the world causing chaos and confusion. Who would be on board? How many could fit?

He never answered those questions. Instead, he had already pre-determined the people who'd join him when it left the surface, the rest forced to deal with the propaganda machines that told them they were remaining behind for a purposeful reason.

The corrupt left behind the just.

When it was announced that the final cache of war heads would be detonated to prevent future instances and unexpected explosions, the people had no choice but to smile and nod. Accept their fates.

Huddle in the basement, in the fallout shelters and wish upon a star that they survived.

*

33. Silo

Morning brought confusion, then sorrow.

At first, he forgot where he was.

Remembering.

He had spent the night in the school.

Remembering.

Percival and Raj.

Thompson. Scum almost equal to Eldridge.

Harkins walked to the doors of the school, body stiff from both his time in the hiding place and the night spent on the cot. He expected to open them and be met by a group of soldiers.

Instead it was a fog-covered morning as he stepped out into the world and began to walk back towards the place he called home.

He stayed alert, slinking along the streets like a snake leaving its den after hibernation. At each intersection he paused, making sure the coasts were clear before crossing.

To his surprise, when he made it back to his house he found the door closed. Entering, he smiled finding that the soldiers hadn't broken in, hadn't destroyed the place.

Looking towards the beach, he wondered how he'd be able to complete the mission. Thompson had shared the plan. It had been his idea, but it was all a ruse. But it was a *good* plan. Harkins wouldn't return to the industrial bay ever again, but what he had seen was a real device. He was confident that Thompson had been telling the truth there. Pen to paper was the next logical step. Harkins would need to visit the silo and look at the structure to get a good idea of what this task would entail.

Walking towards the study in the back of the house, the creak of a floorboard stopped him in his tracks. Somebody else was here.

He looked for a weapon, anything of substance to protect himself with and found an old bowling trophy. He twisted and broke the bowling pin from the base, happy to feel some heft, and stepped to the door.

Pushing it open, he held the pin up high, but lowered it as soon as he saw who was standing in the room.

Two short men stood at the far side of the room. Their heads were heavily bandaged, as were their hands.

"Who are you?" Harkins asked, looking to confirm it was just the two of them.

"Are you Harkins? We're workers at the silo. Raj sent us a letter. He said we can trust Harkins."

He smiled. Thompson had been a Returner, but Raj had been truthfully wanting revenge.

"I am Harkins."

"We haven't much time."

34.

The silo was a strange thing to Harkins. The shape, the space within. Roberts and Richards, the two who'd been hiding in the house, shared how Eldridge had built the structure shortly before the revolving ship had left. It was designed to host the orb machine and as such the interior was laid out to accommodate just that.

"We have two days until the Returners are back. Thompson is pissed that they couldn't find you. Sounds like Eldridge himself gave Thompson the surveillance instructions."

"How long's Thompson been undercover?"

"We think from day one. We never fully trusted him. Raj. Raj was different. He cared about us. He brought us food and water. Bandages."

Harkins could see Roberts was fighting to not cry. He placed a hand on the man's shoulder, making sure not to pull away when he felt only a bony joint under his palm. These two were maybe five feet tall. Harkins didn't want to think what they weighed. Malnourishment was obviously something that'd be occurring on the surface, but this was starvation.

He sniffed, offered Harkins a smile and walked ahead.

"So, here's how the machine works. We shovel the solution from this pit into this chamber, it heats up in this chamber, gets forced into the tubes, travels up and up and voila – orbs."

"Do you know what the solution is?"

"No, we don't," Richards said, standing near the empty pit. "Empyrean manufactures it onboard the ship, transports it down. It fills the pit and when the harp sounds, we begin shovelling."

"What needs to be done?"

"We need to determine what to put in the orbs now and when the Returners arrive, get rid of Matthison."

"Who is Matthison?"

"An Eldridge servant who is in charge of launching the orbs."

"I've figured out what to put in the orbs. The old school has the basics of the chemicals, but I'll need larger volumes."

"There's a factory near the edge of town that was used to produce pharmaceutical grade chemicals. We can make a trip there and stock up."

The plan was in place. Harkins felt elated. He didn't care about what would happen to the students who were selected to jump. This was about exacting revenge on Eldridge and letting that tyrant know Harkins was still down here.

35.

Harkins and his two new friends clicked immediately and worked together to get everything ready to execute their sabotage.

An old man with a weak leg and his two pals who were half the size of any of the Returners. It didn't matter. They were going to show Empyrean that they meant business.

They'd gathered enough of the chemicals to make a fair sized batch of Harkins solution. No better way to test it out than on the soldiers when they returned to the silo.

Harkins, Richards and Roberts had rigged up scaffolding with a wide tray that sat above the entrance to the structure. When Matthison and his two helpers entered, they'd wait a moment before dumping the solution from above. This would allow themselves to watch from a safe distance and see what happened while also remaining out of harm's way.

Patience was the key, and when the door opened below and to their delight and surprise they saw Matthison, Thompson and the two workers enter, Harkins held his hand up. Roberts and Richards remained still, watching for the moment when that hand dropped.

"We've searched for him, but he's gone underground. Eldridge is pissed. Hell, even Jack is pissed. Harkins will pop his head up again. We have some time until the next Salvation event. We'll find him before then," Thompson spoke. Once he was done, Harkins let out a whistle getting all of their attentions. At the same moment, he dropped his hand and the two tipped the barrel housing the solution over.

The four below had no time to react, the chemical mixture splashing down on them. All four began to scream, but that didn't last long, their pains drowned out as the solution dissolved through them, creating little pools of remains that bubbled and hissed.

Seeing it happen, Harkins felt a mix of emotions; guilt over the reality of having taken four lives but also excitement over it actually working.

"You saw what they did to Raj and Percival. They would do the same to us," Roberts said, beginning to climb down the scaffolding.

He had a point, but Harkins still had a rock in his stomach.

"So, did the solution meet your standards?" Richards asked, once they were all standing around the remains on the floor.

"No. I'll need a higher concentration of one key chemical. We need to have instant evaporation. I don't want any trace left behind."

The trio spoke of what to do next, of how things would happen from here. Richards left the silo to deliver a message to the pilot of the transport vessel. They'd return to the revolving ship to pass on that message to Eldridge. They were confident that with Matthison and Thompson eliminated, Eldridge would take time to plot Empyrean's response. The town was of minimal importance to Eldridge. Bigger cities further in land with larger silos had been under construction for some time, the desire and need to finish them pushed aside as the number of inhabitants on the ship diminished. Eldridge could simply change course and launch the orbs elsewhere. But Harkins knew, that as long as he was alive, that wouldn't be the case. Eldridge wanted Harkins to suffer.

Harkins had long wondered what the solution had been within the orbs. Now, he realized he had a chance to examine it in great detail, as the delivery had been made, if not co-opted by their actions. He instructed Richards and Roberts to transport the containers left behind to the school.

He'd hole up there working on his own solution while experimenting on what Eldridge had created.

36. Solution

Early morning sun warmed Harkins old bones as he limped through town. The school brought him such joy each day as he worked closer and closer to unlocking Eldridge's secret.

He had been hesitant to touch the solution at first, but when tools and different things he placed into some of the viscous material didn't dissolve or magically disappear, he tentatively stuck a finger into it. When nothing happened he realized a missing ingredient was how the solution worked to absorb the selected jumpers. An accelerant. Was it due to the speed of the jumper and the heat upon impact?

He tried to write out equations on the chalk board, but from years of disuse, the chalk would crack and crumble. Harkins instead had to resort to writing the equations in his mind. It was on one such morning that it came to him. The velocity of the jumper when impacting with the orb that was also travelling towards them created an equal and opposite force transference. Coupled with the heat that both objects had created, multiplied by the atmosphere around it meant only one thing.

"Discovering their future," he said to the empty room. It was genius if not daunting. Eldridge had a mind like no other. The man was capable of anything and everything.

But this also made him feel like he had the upper hand now. Eldridge firmly believed that he was selecting the jumpers for Salvation. He understood that when they jumped, they'd catch their orb and be transported elsewhere. Harkins was ready to change that. No longer would the selected be saved by the solution. Now, when they leaped and caught their orb, they'd be dissolved, instantly removed from existence. A big, massive middle finger to Eldridge, Empyrean and Morton. He grew contemplative then, wondering how Morton and her adopted child were doing. A part of him wished he was still in that inner circle, laughing with all of them on the Royal Level.

The day was turning to night outside of the school. Harkins was always surprised with how fast time would move when he was deep in thought.

He left the building, stopping to stare at the twinkling stars above him.

He always searched for the larger, brighter shine of the revolving ship, thinking to all of those years he spent looking down on the planet from above.

*

"Empyrean, Empyrean – for the greater good of man,

Empyrean, Empyrean – each citizen does what they can!

For the future, for the ship, we hold our head's up high,

We work as hard as we can – Empyrean we do rely!"

They sang the song with smiles, their muscles aching.

"Break!" the foreman hollered.

He took her hand, leading here down to the water and out onto the dock. She kissed his cheek, as they sat with legs crossed.

Looking out towards the edge of the world, he leaned over, head resting on her shoulder.

"I can't do this much longer," he said, keeping his voice low so that the soldiers who kept watch wouldn't hear.

"Me neither. But we don't have a choice."

"But we do," he said, uncrossing his legs and letting them dip into the water. The pain was immediate.

"Citizen, legs out of the water, now!" the soldier shouted, running down the wood dock towards them.

"It'll only hurt for a moment," he said, taking her hand. She smiled and let him pull her into the water.

The soldier arrived two seconds after, but it was already too late.

Laying twelve feet below him on the lake floor were two skeletons, their embrace visible from where he stood.

*

37. The Visit

The following morning, Harkins meditated.

He'd been trying to fit it in most days, once he realized he was starting to have memory issues.

He'd no longer enjoyed walking to Grey, worried he'd forget where he was or why he was in the middle of nowhere, now reliant on Richards and Roberts to fetch him supplies as needed.

On the morning when things took a strange turn, Harkins had went to the end of the dock, sitting down with care. He couldn't bring himself to look into the clear depths, knowing he'd see the skeletons. He often wondered what the story was with those two, a dozen feet below.

Ten minutes into some visualization and focused breathing, he heard footsteps coming down the dock behind him. Expecting Richards or Roberts, he ignored the approach, drifting back to his visualizations. For this session he was focusing on what the orbs may look like travelling through the atmosphere, going higher and higher.

The footsteps stopped directly behind him, the person's body blocking the sun and putting Harkins into a shadow.

"I'm almost done," Harkins said.

"Doctor Edward Harkins," a man whom he didn't recognize said. Harkins turned his head, seeing an Empyrean Returner.

"Yes, what may I do for you?"

He tried to remain as calm as possible, doing his best to shield his face from the brightness of the sun and not show any fear.

"Mr. Eldridge has requested a meeting."

"He does, does he?"

"He understands that you're in no position to travel to the ship and he doesn't wish to have you return. So, he's sent me to let you know he'll be here tomorrow. He's requested your presence at a place that he's sure you'll find fair and safe."

"Here," he replied without a second thought. It'd be open, no chance of ambush and Richards and Roberts could come along.

"Tomorrow," the soldier said with a nod, turning and making his way back up the dock. Beyond the departing man Harkins could see four other Empyrean soldiers standing at the end of the dock. He hadn't even heard them arrive. It made him wonder how they travelled so quietly.

He waited until the soldiers had disappeared through the streets of the town. While curious he had no desire to see where they'd landed or how they travelled. He presumed it was a ship similar to the one he'd been jettisoned on, but he knew Eldridge was always working on something.

Instead, he went to the silo, in search of Richards and Roberts. Some days they slept on the hard floor of the building, other days they'd find refuge in one of the nearby abandoned houses. Harkins knew they had a place somewhere in Grey, but it was a long trip, so sometimes it was easier for them to spend the night.

He was glad to hear them bickering inside. The constant back and forth between them made him chuckle repeatedly each day.

Entering, the two went silent.

"Eldridge is coming tomorrow," he said.

"Here?" Roberts replied.

"Yes. He wants to discuss something. We'll meet at the beach near the dock. I'd like you both to be there. I don't believe we have anything to fear."

Harkins left them to debate whether they should be worried. He returned to the school, deciding to continue focusing on trying to crack the chemical code for the substance within the orbs. He'd long ago hypothesized the exterior coating was a silicon derivative, which could be easily synthesized, even on this godforsaken planet, but the stuff *within* – that continued to stump him.

While he worked, the afternoon gave way to evening, Harkins decided to call it for the night and return to his home.

It wasn't until he'd closed the door behind him and entered his kitchen that anxiety began to take hold. He'd told Roberts and Richards that he didn't believe they had anything to fear, but now, standing in the chaos that was once a family home, he wasn't so sure he believed that.

38.

Much to Harkins chagrin, soldiers had already arrived when the three of them arrived at the dock. As they approached, the soldiers parted, revealing a man sitting in a motorized wheelchair.

Harkins let out an audible gasp when he realized that the man sitting before them was Eldridge.

"Harkins," he said, his skin so pale that the movement of blood through the capillaries was visible.

"What in the hell happened to you, Eldridge?"

The two smiled at each other as old friends often do. The hurt and horror that had occurred between them momentarily pushed aside, forgotten in that instance.

"I've made many mistakes," he said, eyes falling to Harkins leg. "Which is why I'm here today."

"Morton know you're here?" he asked. He wanted a little insight into where she ranked in the Empyrean Empire now.

"She's been gone for... many years," Eldridge said, his face flashing something resembling pain for a second. "I couldn't save her."

Harkins was taken back. Morton was dead. How was that possible?

"I see how it is. You chose her over me and now with her gone, you need me once again to try and aid you in your quest for immortality? That was always the end goal, wasn't it?"

"It was and is. No, this is something else entirely. Morton was able to open up many doors with different experiments. But, like I said, I need your help fixing a mistake."

"Which is?"

"You were against Morton adopting from the Ward Level. In two months, a class that has been selected for Salvation will jump. I know you've been trying to sabotage the orbs. I'm going to help you. I need you to eradicate the entire class. Do this, and you just may find yourself having returned into my favor and residing on the ship once again."

Harkins looked at Richards and Roberts. He could tell from their faces that they didn't trust what Eldridge was saying. But at the same time, Harkins was intrigued. He had no vested interest in those jumpers. It was the last part that intrigued him but also made him wonder how much he *could* trust Eldridge.

"I'd return to the ship?"

"You would."

"And my leg would be fixed."

"You have my word."

"And I'd be researching again?"

"Yes."

Harkins took a step forward, the soldiers raising their weapons, but Eldridge waved them back.

Harkins extended his hand, Eldridge reciprocating and the two shook.

They'd begin work immediately, the man in the chair said, urging Harkins to follow.

As they made their way through the streets towards the school, Harkins took a look at the sky, wondering if that really was where he wanted his future to be.

39. Arrival

Hunched over the device, Harkins smiled watching the modified orbs launch high above. They sped along, travelling higher and higher before he'd see a small flash of orange and be filled with glee that another of the Empyrean Chosen were snuffed out.

What happened when you caught your orb?

He often wondered that, wondered just where the person would be transported. Eldridge had shared a little with Harkins in their meetings leading up to Salvation Day.

Harkins had sat completely silent while listening to his former friend and colleague share intricate and in-depth details about the development of the orbs and the hypothesis of what happened when a student successfully was absorbed.

"But that's not what I want. Not this time," Eldridge had said, slamming a frail palm on the cracked desk at the school.

He thought of just how deranged Eldridge had sounded as he shared his desire to have Harkins send up modified orbs, but he didn't put much stock in it. Harkins cared more about finding a way back onto the ship. That would allow him to regain Eldridge's complete trust and he'd be able to exact some revenge on the Empyrean scum who'd taken everything from him.

So deep in thought while Roberts and Richards shovelled the new substance into the machine, that he never heard the door open behind him, nor did he hear the approach of footsteps.

"Excuse me?"

All three jumped and whirled around, surprised to see someone standing in the silo.

"Who the hell are you?" Harkins asked.

"I'm Lizzie. Who are you?"

Harkins got off the chair, shuffling towards the intruder. Something was off with them, something that felt familiar.

"I'm Dr. Harkins. Where did you come from? You are new to me. To here." His head bobbed around, inspecting Lizzie up and down, side to side.

"I'm from the ship. I jumped, caught my orb, but instead of being absorbed I landed on Earth."

Harkins, Roberts and Richards gasped in surprise, staring at Lizzie.

"The revolving ship? You're a star person?"

"I guess."

"Are you Empyrean scum?"

"Pardon?"

"If you're from where you claim you are, you must be Empyrean scum, yes? Mr. Eldridge work his claws into why you're up there and we're down here? Scraping and fighting for morsels of uncontaminated food that he sends when the occasion suits him."

"I was a student. Our class was selected to jump for our future."

"Ahh, haha. Yes. The orbs. The future. Nothing but rubbish. Each orb is filled with my concoction now, you see. Molten-acid, I'm afraid. Our way of giving back to the vengeful God that lords above us in his ship. In your case, we simply failed. Sadly you lived."

Lizzie's eyes went wide.

Harkins could see they were fighting back tears. *Had they lost someone to his sabotaged orbs?*

"But Jack told me he'd jumped before?"

"Ha! Jack Eldridge?" Harkins spit a dark-green gob to the floor, where it sizzled upon impact. Wiping some sweat from his forehead, he continued. "He'll say whatever needs to be said to keep his spot on that ship. Such a grotesque thing he is. He delivers our food from time to time. He'll even give us more if we find his addictions for him. Real piece of work, that man."

Lizzie looked at Harkins, the device, the two men still holding their shovels. Was Lizzie going to run? They looked ready to bolt back out the door. This could be an opportunity, though. Harkins knew he needed to act fast, reassure them that they were on the same team, on the same page.

"I can see you're realizing what I've said is true. How you survived, beats me. But you did. You wanted a future. Maybe I can offer one for you?"

Lizzie's eyes flashed with rage. Harkins stifled a smile, seeing the connection.

He stepped towards Lizzie, one of the bandages coming loose, fluttered, exposing the open sores beneath, the charred skin surrounding it. He made no effort to fix it, to hide his wounds. He wanted Lizzie to trust him, to see him vulnerable.

"This can't be true," was all Lizzie could manage.

"My dear, I'm afraid it is. Look around. Look at what man did to this planet. To this town. We fight and we battle for every day of our existence."

"And you would offer me a future?"

"Absolutely."

"Why?"

"Because, you're from up there. You know things."

He watched Lizzie mull what he'd said over, hoping that somehow he'd been convincing enough to be seen as an ally and potentially a friend.

"Where do we begin?"

He smiled, happy that he'd been able to persuade Lizzie.

"I'm so pleased, Lizzie. Come, my new friend. Let's make a place for you. One that will give you everything you always wanted."

They walked back over to the device, as Roberts and Richards began to shovel solution into the chamber. The sound of the solution being formed echoed, Lizzie watching the sequence with astonishment.

As an orb was blasted far above them, Lizzie tapped Harkins on the shoulder, getting his attention.

"Yes?"

"How did you learn how this all worked?"

"Eldridge. The man told me his secrets himself."

Lizzie nodded. Harkins could tell that there was significant distrust but he'd push on.

This was his chance.

Eldridge believed Harkins was eradicating all of the chosen students for Salvation. Lizzie believed Harkins wanted to exact revenge on Eldridge.

In the end, Harkins would find a way back onto the ship, which would mean collateral damage.

"So, tell me Lizzie. Any family still on the ship?"

The device chimed again, an orb launching.

"Two more to go," Roberts called out.

"No," Lizzie replied.

"I'm sorry to hear. I've been off the ship for some time, I wouldn't even recognize half of the research team anymore."

"Last one," Richards called out, as they scooped the final bit of solution from the pit and shovelled it into the chamber.

"Come, I'll show you my place and we'll find one for yourself," Harkins said. "Meet us at the house," he called to Roberts and Richards.

Lizzie followed Harkins as they made their way slowly from the silo. The town looked different to them, Harkins watching as Lizzie took in what was now home.

"You look so familiar," he said, struggling to place why he sensed a familiarity about Lizzie.

"Maybe you worked with my mom?"

"Possibly. Who was your mom?"

"Rachel Morton," Lizzie said, not noticing Harkins shoulders bunch up towards his neck.

"Hmmm, can't say I'm familiar with that name," Harkins lied, forcing himself to not turn and club Lizzie to death with his cane.

"Here we are," he said instead, arriving at his broken down house.

Lizzie smiled, nodded, walked up the steps.

Harkins followed, pushing the door open and waited for his guest to enter.

His head was spinning.

Had Eldridge sent Lizzie to spy on him? Had Lizzie actually jumped and somehow survived the sabotage? If they really were Morton's daughter that meant their blood was valuable. Or had things changed? Harkins didn't know, but now alarm bells were ringing even as they smiled at each other and

Lizzie walked around the living room inspecting his notes and books.

"Please, have a seat. I want you to be comfortable," he said, motioning for the dusty couch. Lizzie went over and sat, watching the man putter and mumble to himself.

An uneasy trust had been formed immediately, but now the atmosphere had shifted subtlety. Something was bothering them both, something that sat just below the surface, neither able to speak it out loud.

For Harkins, the door that had seemingly opened was now half shut, the reality that Eldridge may have sent a spy to see his true intentions caused his anger to boil.

For Lizzie, they were unsure as to how much they could trust this little man and whether he was a friend of Eldridge's or not.

"Tomorrow, we'll walk to Grey, the city nearby. Tomorrow, you can help me begin our plan to get back onto the ship and take out Eldridge. But tonight, I'll make us some soup and you can relax. You've had a long day."

Lizzie nodded, their eyes drooping as they sat.

Harkins hoped Lizzie dozed off soon, so he could gather his wits.

His future had changed once again. Eldridge seemed to be able to continue to mess with the playing deck, throw curveballs at Harkins, but this time... this time Harkins was prepared for the deception and the reality that Lizzie was on Eldridge's team. If Lizzie even moved in the wrong way or spoke highly of Eldridge, there would be consequences. Immediate and severe.

As Lizzie began to lightly snore, Harkins sat and tried to relax.

Tomorrow, they'd walk to Grey and he'd find the space Eldridge had described. Under one of the monuments to his glory, sat a device that would be most beneficial. A device that would aid Harkins and help to devour the ones that got in his way.

END

To be continued in...
The Devourers: Book Three of the Empyrean Saga

About the Author

Steve Stred is the Splatterpunk Nominated Author of 'Sacrament' and 'Mastodon.'

Based in Edmonton, Alberta, Canada, Steve has released over a dozen novels and novellas as well as a number of collections. He has appeared alongside some of horror's biggest names within some truly excellent anthologies.

He is a proud co-founder of the LOHF Writer's Grant and an Active Member of the HWA.

Website: stevestredauthor.wordpress.com

Twitter: @stevestred

Instagram: @stevestred

Books: author.to/stevestred

www.ingramcontent.com/pod-product-compliance
Lightning Source LLC
Chambersburg PA
CBHW051808050726
47598CB00006B/2479